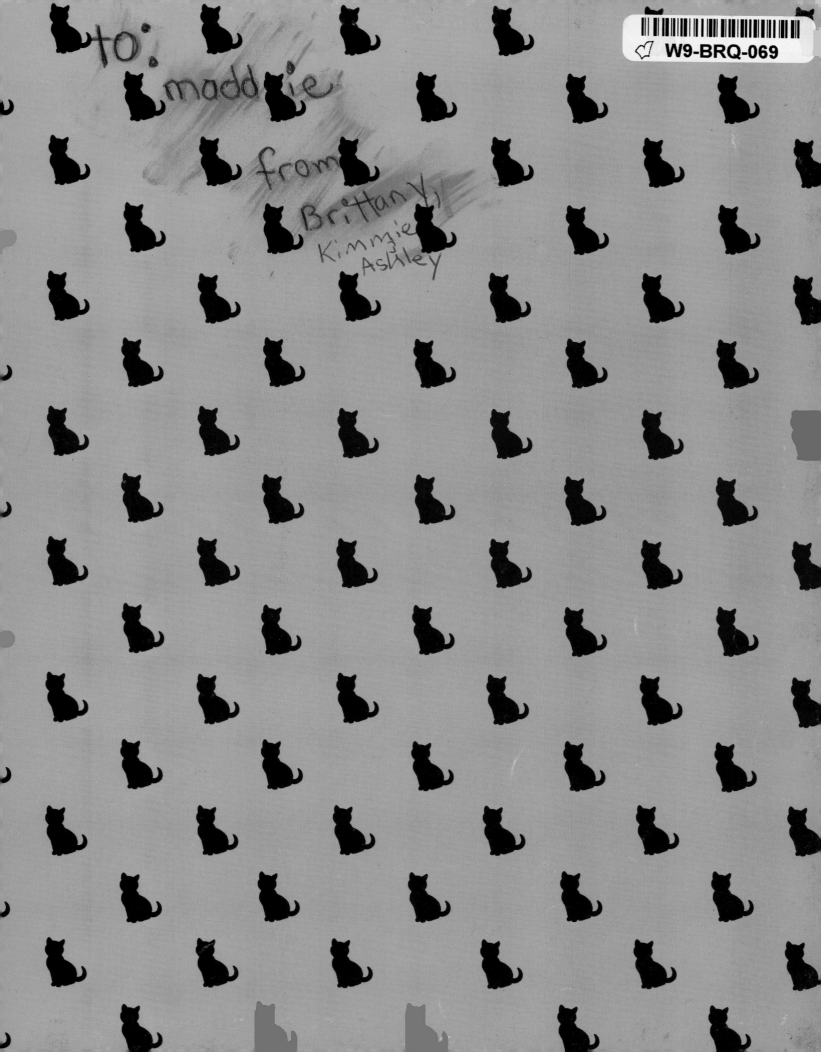

to: maddie

from Brittany,
Kimmie
Ashley

This 1988 edition published by Derrydale Books
Distributed by Crown Publishers, Inc.
225 Park Avenue South, New York, New York 10003
Printed and Bound in Italy

ISBN 0-517-66782-7

hgfedcba

WHO WANTS TO ADOPT

WILLY
THE WANDERING
KITTEN

Derrydale Books

New York

Willy was weary of watching his brother always chasing butterflies and of seeing his other brother always napping.

Mother cat never moved-she was always stretched out, keeping a watchful eye on her kittens.

From the day he was born, three months before, Willy had set out to explore the world around him.

As soon as he was able to totter on four legs, he left the safety of his mother's soft fur. Little by little, he scampered farther away, looking around the big garden. First, he climbed onto a tub with a rose bush. But when the thorns pricked him, he ran crying back to Mother. And her warm, loving tongue licked away the pain of the little stabs. His next adventure was with the pail. When he scrambled inside, it toppled over on its side with a loud noise.

This time, the sudden fall, as much as the noisy clatter, frightened Willy. But, when he rushed home to Mother for sympathy, she was a little less comforting than usual.

Willy knew everything about the garden, since the garden was surrounded by a high wooden fence his roaming was limited. The house was close by but the door was never open. Mother cat had firmly warned her kittens. "None of you must ever go into the house! There are people inside!"

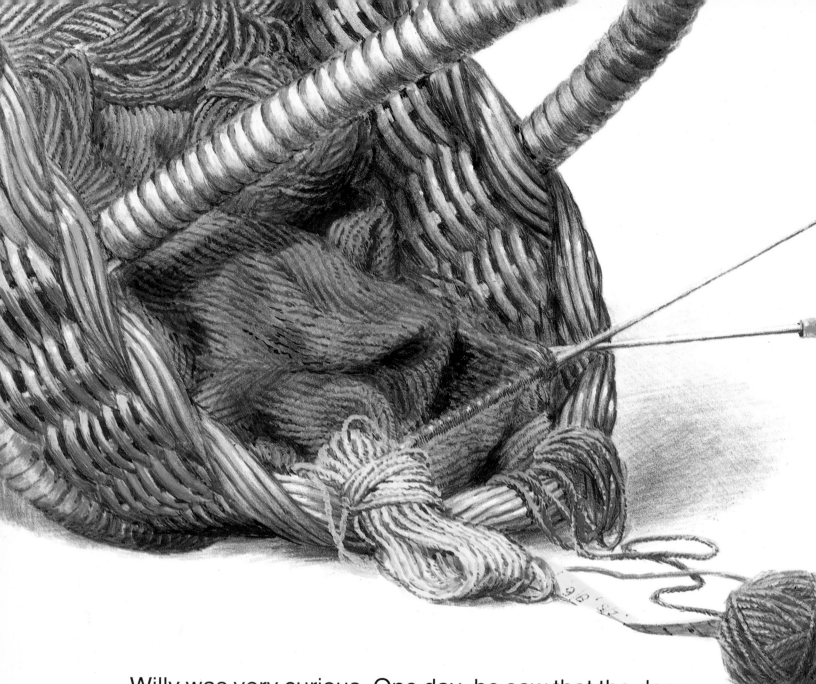

Willy was very curious. One day, he saw that the door was open. He completely forgot his mother's warnings and entered to explore a new world.

How different it was from the familiar garden! His little paws slipped on the smooth floor, the furniture towered high and there was a strange new smell.

"That must be the smell of people!" said the kitten to himself. His paws overturned a basket that had caught his eye. Now he discovered a splendid new game. The balls of wool scattered over the floor as the kitten poked them. Then he chased them.

"I wonder why Mommy wouldn't allow us to come in here? Now, this is *fun*! There's nothing like this in the garden!"

But the long yellow measuring tape wouldn't play with Willy.
The harder the kitten tried to make it run, the more it just flopped around him. What a disappointment! Willy felt alarmed when he heard footsteps and quickly hid under the furniture, as a woman's voice scolded.

"Who upset the wool basket? Have the cats gotten in?"
And a stiff broom was shoved under the furniture, hunting for the intruder. It brushed past the kitten, huddled in a far corner.

"Now, that's odd! No cats here!"
Still grumbling, the woman picked up the wool basket and left the room.

Willy hid for a long time. He was afraid.

He didn't know what the woman had said, but he was sure he had been in great danger.
As time passed, his courage returned. Very cautiously, he crept from his hiding place.

No danger in sight! The kitten returned to play with the
basket, but by then he was tired of that game. Next, he began
to look round for something else to do.
    Just then he noticed that the woman had left the door open.

The next room was dimly lit, but he could see in the dark. Willy's curiosity was aroused by a large bowl in the center of the table. He stared at the two fish swimming nervously inside. Then he dipped a paw into the water. The poor little fish were terrified. But Willy was too small to move the bowl or knock it over. Willy wanted to grab the fish moving in the water. The fish were very sure that the kitten was dangerous.

They stared at each other for a long time, with the bowl between them, until they almost became friends. The big fish even swam near the kitten's paw, on the other side of the glass.

"Cro, croo, crooo!" sang a pair of parakeets, in a cage hidden by a big black curtain.

Willy turned around, trying to find out who was making the sound. Then he slipped under the curtain and found the birds.

"Oh, how pretty!" he said to himself, admiring their bright feathers.

"Cro, croo, crooo!" sang the parakeets, paying no attention to the kitten.

"They're so happy! Anyone can see they're in love!"

Then Willy spotted the wire of the cage, and though he went right around it, he could see no opening.

"They must be shut in!" he decided. That made him feel

even happier than the parakeets, since *he* could roam wherever he liked. By this time, the kitten had explored every room with an open door. The only place unexplored was the cellar, at the bottom of a long flight of dark steps. It was difficult for the small kitten to scramble down such high steps. However, when he reached the bottom, he was excited to see a mouse scamper past.

Once he had recovered from the surprise, Willy dashed after the mouse, but did not notice a huge spider's web hanging across his path.

The slender but tough threads stuck to his coat, and the harder he struggled to free himself, the more he became tangled in the web. Luckily, as he twisted and turned, his paws never once touched the trap that the mouse had also escaped.

He could still feel the bits of that nastry web on his soft fur, and he rubbed himself along the floor to scrape away every trace. All Willy wanted now was to get out!

A little window above a pile of big boxes seemed to be the best way of escaping from the cellar. And soon the kitten was out in the front yard.

There lay a large dog, dozing beside an empty dish. Willy very interested, padded over.

"Well! He doesn't look nearly as bad as Dad said! But he is a dog all right! He is wearing a collar, just as they said!"

Now the dog, one eye closed and the other fixed on Willy, watched the kitten approach. At one point, Willy poked into the dog's hairy ear. The dog grumpily raised his head and yawned. The dog's huge mouth and long teeth frightened Willy.

"Oh, dear! What awful jaws!"

So off he strolled to the other end of the dog, where the tail twitched lazily. Willy playfully tried to grab the tail each time it twitched. For a while, the dog let the kitten play his little game, but when Willy tried to *bite* the tail, the dog rose to his feet and barked noisily.

Willy ran off in terror.

That is how he met Hedgehog. Nobody had ever told him about such an animal. Actually, he met a baby hedgehog who was more or less his own age. The youngster was patiently waiting for a large worm that had vanished dawn a hole to return.

The kitten went over to the hedgehog and asked:

"What are you doing?"

The baby hedgehog replied:

"A large worm has gone down this hole. Sooner or later he's going to reappear and then he'll turn into my lunch."

Willy shuddered, but went on:

"You're not a cat. Nor a dog! And you're not a mouse! Just what are you?"

"What?! Don't you know? I'm a hedgehog! I eat mice!"

Willy stared in wonder at the little animal facing him.

"How can you eat mice? I've just seen one, nearly as big as you! And I thought you said you eat worms."

"I eat worms because I'm only a baby, but when I grow up to be like Mom and Dad, then I'll switch to mice."

"Cats eat mice, too. But I love milk, don't you?"

"Yes, I like milk, but my Mom says I'm big now, so I must get used to other kinds of food."

Meanwhile, as the two friends chattered away, the worm wriggled unseen from his hole and well out of danger.

Willy lifted a paw to pat his new friend, but Hedgehog's spines pricked his tender skin. With a squeak of pain, he hastily withdrew his paw.

Indeed, on hearing the kitten's cry, Mother Hedgehog appeared to see what was happening.

The second she spied the kitten, she hunched her back and rolled up into a prickly ball, telling her son to do the same. And all poor Willy could do, in spite of his friendly intentions, was to drift away unhappily.

Having left the hedgehog, Willy headed for a large nearby field. He was watching a bee buzz over a clump of daisies, when he felt himself lifted into the air.

"What's this pretty kitten doing here without its Mommy?" said a boy, as he stroked Willy.

"You're so soft. What a sweet little face!"

Now, nobody had ever petted Willy so nicely before, and he was so pleased he closed his eyes and purred.

"Purr! Purr!" he rumbled, in the boy's arms.

"There! Stay on the fence and don't budge! If you wait there while I see to the ponies hay, and if you're good, I'll take you home and give you a nice bowl of milk."

So Willy perched on the wooden fence, watching the pony and her foal. How friendly they looked! Though they were much bigger than Willy, the kitten was not afraid, for he knew they meant no harm. After a while, tired of clinging in an awkward position, Willy jumped from the fence and rolled onto the grass.

Already, he had forgotten the boy's caresses and was ready to continue with his interesting travels.

"Meow! Meow!" What a long time since he last heard that familiar cry! Looking up, he saw a kitten of his own age on the roof of the house. But this kitten was black as coal, with a white waistcoat.

"Meow!" called Willy cheerfully. The mother cat on the roof turned around to see who had spoken.

"Meow! Meow!" she cried, "Where have you come from?"

"Meow!" replied Willy, "I live with my Mommy and my brothers in the garden near here. Can I come up beside you?"

"Meow! Meow!" agreed the two black kittens.

It was quite frightful getting up the tree leading to the roof, but at last Willy succeeded in reaching his new friend.

The kittens said "hello" gently by rubbing their pink noses together. Then they took off to explore the rooftops.

"Oh, look! What's that?" cried Willy.
"It's a lizard!" replied the black kitten.
"Will it bite?" asked Willy.

"Oh, no! If it sees us, it will run away!" said the black kitten.

"Ssss! Sss!" whispered the black kitten. "The swallows! The babies are alone now. Their parents aren't around!"

Willy gaped at the baby swallows, chirping hungrily with open beaks, while his friend tried, but failed, to reach the nest tucked under the eaves.

"Don't lean out like that! You'll fall. It's dangerous!"

Just then, a dark shadow flashed past, followed by another.

Father and Mother Swallow had come back to their babies.

"Meow! Meow! Blackie! Come down at once! Leave the nest alone! You can't reach it! You'll only fall!" called the mother cat.

"Bye, Willy! I have to go now, Mommy's calling me. Come back soon!"

Willy watched his little friend disappear over the roof, then bent down to see the baby swallows being fed by their parents. Suddenly, he felt homesick for his own Mommy. So he made his was back to the tree.

He hadn't realized how tall it was. Now that he had to climb down the tree again, he felt a little nervous. However, he built up his courage and carefully stepped into the leaves.

From far away came the sound of a familiar voice. Willy meowed as loudly as he could in reply, but the cry came again and again.

"Willy! Willy! Where are you?"

"Mommy! Mommy! I'm here! I'm coming!"

And a little later, mother cat and her kitten were reunited below the tree.

"What a fright you gave me! And how dirty you are! Where have you been? Come here and let me clean you up a bit!"

And as he felt that warm tongue caress him, Willy was far too happy to bother answering. It was just lovely to be home again with his Mommy.

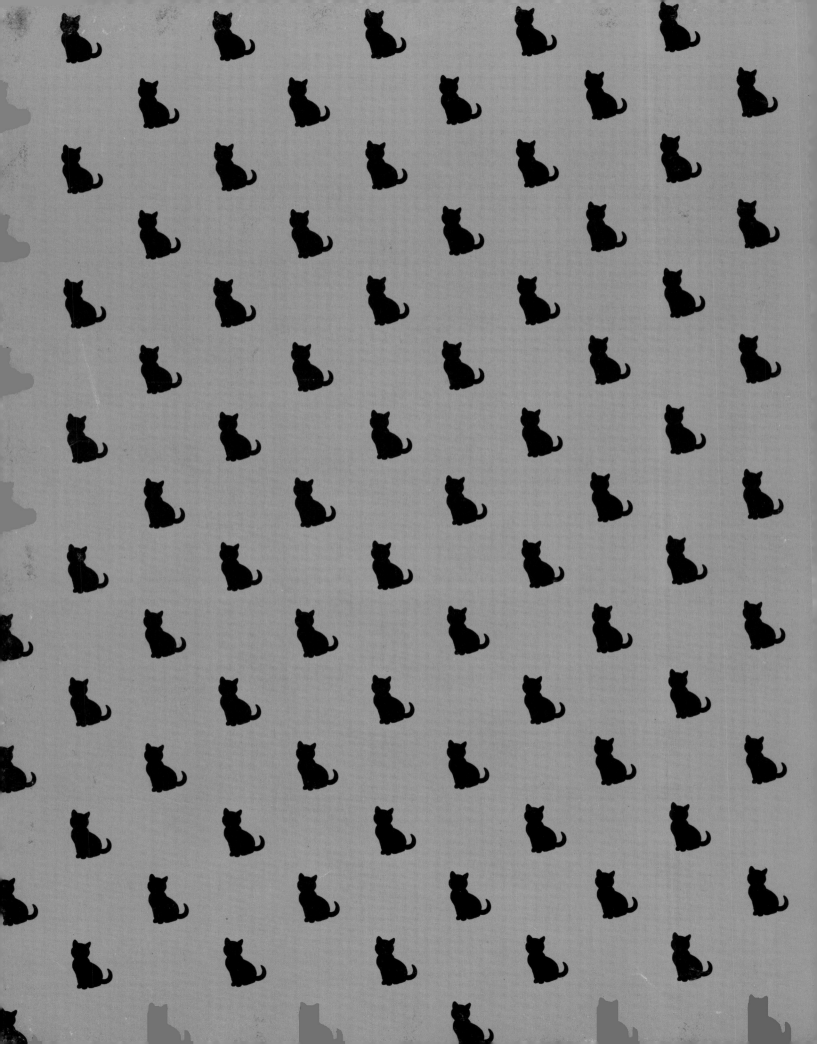